Ladybird  Readers

Who is in the Garden?

To access the audio and digital versions of this book:

1 Go to **www.ladybirdeducation.co.uk**
2 Click "Unlock book"
3 Enter the code below

a8EIR60TK6

Notes to teachers, parents, and carers

The **Ladybird Readers** Beginner level helps young language learners to become familiar with key conversational phrases in English. The language introduced has clear real-life applications, giving children the tools to hold their first conversations in English.

This book focuses on asking and answering questions with the structure "Is there . . .?" and provides practice of naming different animals in English. The pictures that accompany the text show a range of animals, which may be used to introduce some pieces of topic-based vocabulary, such as "sheep" and "dog", if the children are ready.

There are some activities to do in this book. They will help children practice these skills:

 Speaking    Listening*   Writing   Reading   Singing*

*To complete these activities, listen to the audio downloads available at www.ladybirdeducation.co.uk

 **Aardman**

Series Editor: Sorrel Pitts   Text adapted by Hazel Geatches   Song lyrics by Wardour Studios

LADYBIRD BOOKS
UK | USA | Canada | Ireland | Australia
India | New Zealand | South Africa

Ladybird Books is part of the Penguin Random House group of companies whose addresses can be found at global.penguinrandomhouse.com.
www.penguin.co.uk   www.puffin.co.uk   www.ladybird.co.uk

 Penguin
Random House
UK

First published 2021
001

This book is based on 'Learning Time with Timmy', an English language learning experience for pre-school children including the 'Learning Time with Timmy' courses
© British Council 2015; and the 'Learning Time with Timmy' series © Aardman Animations Ltd 2018.

'Timmy Time' and the character 'Timmy' are trademarks used under licence from Aardman Animations Limited.
'Learning Time with Timmy' is a trademark used under licence from Aardman Animations Limited.
britishcouncil.org/english/timmy

Printed in China
A CIP catalogue record for this book is available from the British Library
ISBN: 978-0-241-44005-6

All correspondence to:
Ladybird Books
Penguin Random House Children's
One Embassy Gardens, 8 Viaduct Gardens, London SW11 7BW

FSC
www.fsc.org
MIX
Paper from
responsible sources
FSC® C018179

Ladybird  Readers

Who is in the Garden?

Based on the Learning Time with Timmy TV series
created in partnership with the British Council

Watch the original episode "Jungle Animals" online.

Picture words

Timmy

Ruffy

Mittens

Stripey

footprints

take a photo

elephant

lion

Timmy and Ruffy are in the garden. They see big footprints.

Is there a big animal in the garden?

Yes, there it is! Timmy takes a photo.

The animal has big ears.
Is it an elephant?

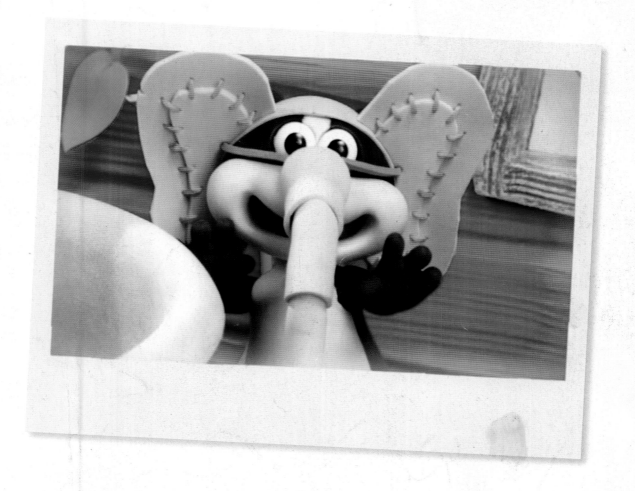

Then, Timmy and Ruffy see
small footprints.

Is there a small animal
in the garden?

Where is it, Ruffy?

14

There it is! Timmy takes a photo.

The animal has yellow hair.
Is it a lion?

No! Who are the animals?
They are Timmy and
Ruffy's friends!

The lion is Mittens. The elephant is Stripey!

Your turn!

1 **Talk with a friend.** 💬

Hello!

Hello!

Who is in the garden?

Timmy and Ruffy.

What does Timmy do?

Timmy takes a photo.

2 Listen and read. Match. 🎧 📖

1 The animal has big ears.

2 Timmy takes a photo.

3 Ruffy and Timmy are in the garden.

4 The lion is Mittens.

3 **Listen. Put a** ✓ **by the words you hear.** 🎧

1 a The animal has big ears. ✓

b The animal has small ears. ☐

2 a Is it an elephant? ✓

b Is it a lion? ☐

3 a The animal has brown hair. ☐

b The animal has yellow hair. ✓

4 a The lion is Timmy! ☐

b The lion is Mittens! ✓

4 **Listen. Write the first letters.** 🎧 ✏️

1 friends

2 lion

3 elephant

5 Sing the song.

Big, big footprints in the garden.
There is a big animal.
The animal has two big, big ears.
Is it an elephant?
There it is! There it is!
Timmy takes a photo!

Small, small footprints in the garden.
There is a small animal.
The animal has yellow, yellow hair.
Is it a lion?
There it is! There it is!
Timmy takes a photo!